For Hazel, Rose, and everyone
at the village school in
Crowhurst — B.M.

For Oliver — G.P.

Text copyright © 2006 by Brian Moses
Illustrations copyright © 2006 by Garry Parsons

First published in the United States of America in 2006 by
Walker Publishing Company, Inc.
Distributed to the trade by Holtzbrinck Publishers

Originally published in the United Kingdom in 2006 by the Penguin Group, Puffin Books

For information about permission to reproduce selections from
this book, write to Permissions, Walker & Company,
104 Fifth Avenue, New York, New York 10011

Library of Congress Cataloging-in-Publication Data
available upon request
ISBN-10: 0-8027-9599-4
ISBN-13: 978-0-8027-9599-1

Visit Walker & Company's Web site at www.walkeryoungreaders.com

Printed in China

2 4 6 8 10 9 7 5 3 1

All papers used by Walker & Company are natural, recyclable products
made from wood grown in well-managed forests. The manufacturing processes
conform to the environmental regulations of the country of origin.

Trouble AT THE DINOSAUR CAFE

Brian Moses
Illustrations by
Garry Parsons

WALKER & COMPANY
New York

Down at the Dinosaur Cafe, everybody was doing fine.

Steggy was slurping his swamp juice,

while
Iggy
sat
down
to dine.

Patty was eating her tree roots and had ordered vegetable pie,

when in
stomped
Tyrannosaurus
with a **wicked**
gleam in his eye.

He read the menu from left to right then **gobbled** it up in one **gulp**.

He chewed upon it
viciously, while the
paper turned
to pulp.

"You plant eaters are fine," he said,
"if that's all you want to eat.
But I'm a **growing** dinosaur

and my stomach **cries** out for **meat.**"

Steggy stiffened,

Iggy trembled,
and Patty fell off her chair.
Tyrannosaurus turned his head
and fixed them with his stare.

I'll add
you

and
YOU

and **YOU!**"

Then hiding behind the counter,
Iggy spoke on her mobile phone,

"Terry Triceratops, please come quick.
We can't handle this on our own."

He **rushed** straight to the cafe and **burst** in through the front doors.

Terry Triceratops, small but **deadly**, fought Tyrannosaurus with ease.

A **whack** and a **Smack** from his three-pronged attack

brought the **big** bully beast to his **knees.**

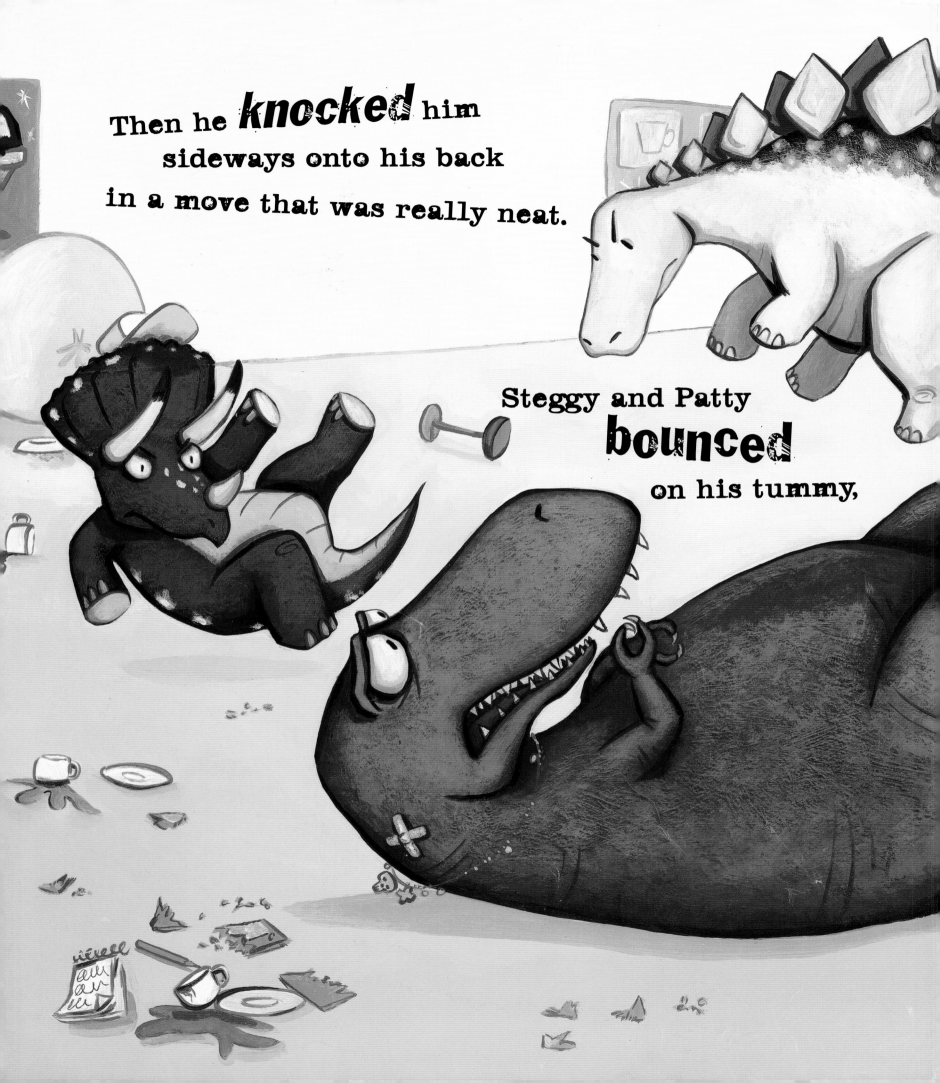

while Iggy **tickled** his feet.

"We'll stop," Steggy said,
   "when you promise
    that you'll stop acting so tough."

"**Anything**," wheezed Tyrannosaurus.
       He was getting quite out of breath.

"And if you break that promise," warned Terry,
      "we'll **tickle** you half to death!"

Tyrannosaurus fled through the doors
in search of easier meat,

while everyone in the Dinosaur Cafe
celebrated his defeat.

But Iggy complained to the others,
"You were okay sitting on his belly.
I had an awful time," she said . . .